After HAPPILY —EVER— AFTER

Snow White
and the Magic Mirror

After Happily Ever After is published by Stone Arch Books
A Capstone Imprint
1710 Roe Crest Drive
North Mankato, Minnesota 56003
www.capstonepub.com

First published by Orchard Books, a division of Hachette Children's Books
338 Euston Road, London NW1 3BH, United Kingdom

Library of Congress Cataloging-in-Publication Data is available
on the Library of Congress website.

ISBN-13: 978-1-4342-7950-7 (hardcover)
ISBN-13: 978-1-4342-7956-9 (paperback)

Summary: Snow White is just TOO nice and always helping other people
out. She never has a moment to herself! She asks her magic mirror for advice
but will she ever really listen to the answer? Snow White must learn to say
no if she's going to live happily ever after...

Designer: Russell Griesmer
Photo Credits: ShutterStock/Maaike Boot, 4, 5, 51

Printed in the United States of America in North Mankato, Minnesota.
032015   008805R

After HAPPILY —EVER— AFTER

Snow White
and the Magic Mirror

by TONY BRADMAN

illustrated by SARAH WARBURTON

STONE ARCH BOOKS®
a capstone imprint

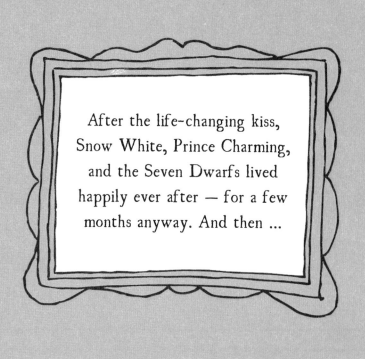

After the life-changing kiss,
Snow White, Prince Charming,
and the Seven Dwarfs lived
happily ever after — for a few
months anyway. And then ...

Snow White was standing in front of an empty canvas with a brush in her hand.

She had been looking forward to this so much! Painting was her passion, although somehow it seemed she could rarely find the time to do it.

Still, she was here now, and in her mind she could see the lovely picture she was going to paint.

But suddenly the door of her studio flew open and in marched her husband, Prince Charming. He was wearing a fancy riding outfit.

"So this is where you've been hiding!" he said. "I've been looking for you everywhere, sweetheart. I wondered if you could do me a teensy tiny favor?"

"Of course, my love," murmured Snow White, chewing the end of her brush as she thought about how to begin her picture. "What do you need me to do?"

"Oh, nothing much," said Prince Charming. "I need you to pick up my dry cleaning, that's all. I forgot, and I'm about to go riding with some friends."

A slight frown crept over Snow White's face. Prince Charming could be very forgetful about doing things like that, and part of her just wanted to start her painting. But another part thought it wouldn't be nice to say no, so she put down her brush and smiled.

"No problem, my love," she said. "You run along and have your fun."

"That's great, thanks!" said the prince as he dashed off. "See you later!"

Snow White left the palace and headed into town. She felt a little miserable, and that made her angry with herself. What right did she have to be unhappy?

Everyone knew her story — the Evil
Stepmother hating her ...

the kind Huntsman letting her live ...

the Seven Dwarfs taking her in ...

the poisoned apple putting her to sleep ...

and the Prince waking her with true love's kiss, which led to their magical wedding.

These days her life was perfect, of course. Although it would be good to have time to paint as well.

There was a lot of dry cleaning to collect and Snow White wondered how she could carry it all. But as she was leaving she noticed a poster on the shop door.

Snow White felt very excited and wrote down all the details. She would love to enter.

GRAND PAINTING
COMPETITION
Prizes to be won!
Deadline for entries –
this Saturday!

But then, as she hurried back to the
palace, her mind began to fill with doubt.
She probably wasn't good enough. Although
maybe she should enter anyway. Soon her
head was spinning with confusion. What
should she do?

She badly needed some advice, and she knew just who to ask — the Magic Mirror! It was the one thing belonging to her stepmother that she had kept.

"Mirror, mirror, on the wall. Should I bother to enter the contest at all?" she asked.

"Go for it, girlfriend! Don't let this pass by," sang the Magic Mirror, its cloudy surface shimmering mysteriously. "Put yourself first, and give it a try."

"I won't know if I come in first unless I enter and win. But thanks, you've helped me make up my mind!" said Snow White. She was confused about the answer but happy for the support.

That night, Snow White found it hard to sleep. She kept thinking about what she was going to paint, and how amazing she wanted it to be.

She was in her studio bright and early the next morning, getting her paints and brushes ready. She was just about to start when her phone rang.

"Hi there, Snow White!" said a deep voice. "I wondered if you could do me a favor. You know I wouldn't normally ask, but we're really desperate."

Snow White's heart sank. She knew instantly the voice belonged to the Huntsman, who was now her friend. He and his wife were lovely people, but they didn't seem to be any good at organizing themselves, which meant they often called Snow White for help.

"I'm not sure I can," said Snow White. "I'm right in the middle of something ..."

"Oh, please, Snow White," said the Huntsman. "Mrs. Huntsman starts a new job today and I'm going to the dentist, so we need you to look after the kids."

Snow White bit her lip. It wouldn't be very nice to say no, would it?

"I'm on my way," she said, putting down her paintbrush with a sigh.

The Huntsman's children were lovely, but they could also be quite lively. Snow White ended up babysitting for most of the day. The Huntsman told an exhausted Snow White that he'd bumped into a friend after he'd left the dentist, and they had lost track of the time.

Snow White would have to wait until tomorrow to start her painting. She slept heavily, and it took her a while to get up and into her studio in the morning. But when she stood in front of the blank canvas, her mind began to fill with doubt once more.

She decided it might be a good idea to have another chat with the Magic Mirror.

"Mirror, mirror, you're so wise," she said. "Do you think I'll win a prize?"

"You could be the best, but not this way," sang the mirror, its surface less cloudy this time, although still shimmering. "Just think of yourself today!"

Snow White frowned. It seemed a strange thing to say, and she went back to staring at her blank canvas. Then suddenly she heard someone knocking at the palace door. She sighed and put down her paintbrush again.

It was Kevin, the youngest of the Seven Dwarfs, and he looked worried.

"Hi, Snow White," he said. "The others have sent me to ask for a favor."

"Don't tell me," said Snow White. "You've had one of your arguments?"

Snow White was fond of the Seven Dwarfs, and she was grateful to them for taking her in. But the one thing she didn't miss about living with them was the constant arguing.

They fought like cats and dogs, and they were always asking her to come by and sort out their fights.

She thought of saying no, but decided that wouldn't be nice. So she went to their house with Kevin and calmed the others down, although it took a while.

The house was a terrible mess, so she spent the rest of the day cleaning up and doing the laundry.

She even cooked them a delicious supper
before she left.

That night, Snow White was very tired and very fed up. She slept badly, and got up in the middle of the night to look at her empty canvas again.

The deadline for the competition was only a couple of days away, and she was no closer to getting her painting finished. In fact, she hadn't even started it!

"Mirror, mirror, tell me true," she murmured as she sat in the moonlight streaming through her window. "Why is this happening? What should I do?"

"I've told you once, I've told you twice," the Magic Mirror sang crossly, its surface totally clear this time. "Face it, girlfriend, you're just TOO nice!"

Snow White looked into the Magic Mirror, and suddenly understood what it had been trying to make her see. She would never get any painting done if she kept putting everybody else first.

She realized it might be time to think of herself, although that would mean saying no, and she didn't know if she could.

Snow White soon had a chance to find out. She was in her studio the next day when Prince Charming came to ask if she would take his library books back for him. They were a year overdue.

"Sorry, sweetheart, I can't," said Snow White. "I'm actually busy."

"Oh, right you are," said the prince,
looking surprised. "Well, not to worry."

Snow White said no a lot over the next two days.

She got her painting done in time for the competition and was very happy when she won!

And strangely enough, once she began
to say no, the people in her life began doing
more for themselves.

Snow White was still nice to everyone, but now she had time to do things she enjoyed as well as helping others. And once that happened, she really did live HAPPILY EVER AFTER!

SNOW WHITE GALLERY

OPENING

ABOUT THE AUTHOR

Tony Bradman writes for children of all ages. He is particularly well known for his top-selling Dilly the Dinosaur series. His other titles include the Happily Ever After series, *The Orchard Book of Heroes and Villains*, and *The Orchard Book of Swords*, *Sorcerers*, and *Superheroes*. Tony lives in South East London.

ABOUT THE ILLUSTRATOR

Sarah Warburton is a rising star in children's books. She is the illustrator of the Rumblewick series, which has been very well received at an international level. The series spans across both picture books and fiction. She has also illustrated nonfiction titles and the Happily Ever After series. She lives in Bristol, England, with her young baby and husband.

GLOSSARY

advice (ad-VICE) — a suggestion about what someone should do

canvas (KAN-vuhss) — a surface for painting made from canvas cloth stretched over a frame

doubt (DOUT) — to feel uncertain

exhausted (eg-ZAWST-ed) — extra tired

murmured (MUR-murd) — talked quietly

shimmering (SHIM-ur-ing) — shining with a faint, flickering light

studio (STOO-dee-oh) — a room or building where an artist or photographer works

surface (SUR-fiss) — the outside of something

DISCUSSION QUESTIONS

1. If you had a talking mirror, what would you ask it?

2. Why was it important for Snow White to take some time for herself?

3. Snow White was a kind person who loved to help others. What kind of job would be good for Snow White? Why?

WRITING PROMPTS

1. Snow White loved to paint. Write about something you love to do.

2. There were many chances for Snow White to politely say no to her friends. Rewrite one of the scenarios from the book with Snow White saying no.

3. Do you think the mirror gave Snow White good advice? Write a paragraph explaining your answer.

THE FUN DOESN'T STOP HERE!